BERNARD
SEES THE WORLD

by Berniece Freschet
Pictures by Gina Freschet

Published by Charles Scribner's Sons, New York

Text copyright © 1976 Berniece Freschet
Illustrations copyright © 1976 Gina Freschet

Library of Congress Cataloging in Publication Data
Freschet, Berniece.   Bernard sees the world.
SUMMARY: Bernard sets out to see the world and ends up seeing the whole
thing—from the moon.
|1. Mice—Fiction.   2. Voyages and travel—Fiction|
1. Freschet, Gina. II. Title.   PZ7.F8896BE |E| 76-1323
ISBN 0-684-14671-1

1 3 5 7 9 11 13 15 17 19 MD/C 20 18 16 14 12 10 8 6 4 2

Printed in the United States of America.

For all adventurers who one day
must see the world.

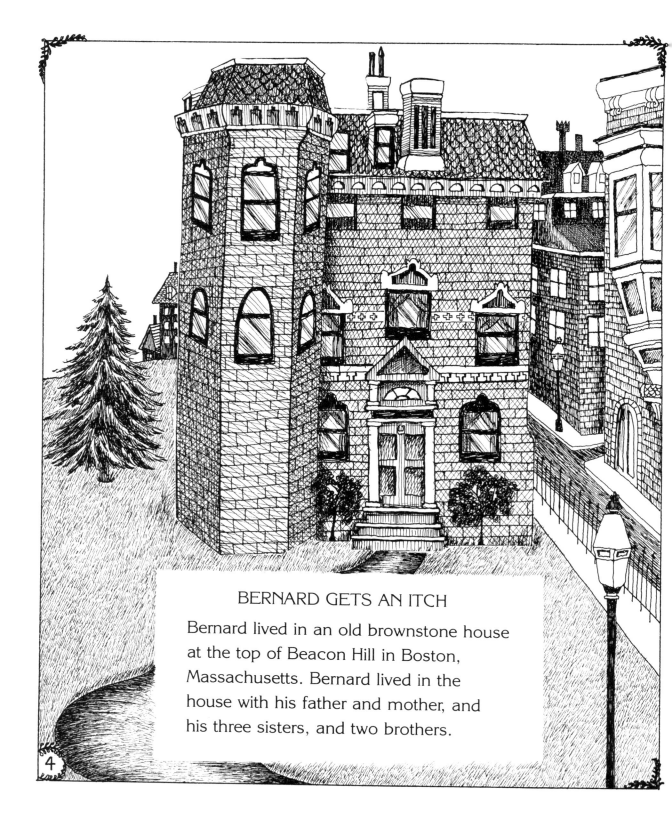

BERNARD GETS AN ITCH

Bernard lived in an old brownstone house
at the top of Beacon Hill in Boston,
Massachusetts. Bernard lived in the
house with his father and mother, and
his three sisters, and two brothers.

4

Bernard's grandparents had lived in this house. And so had his great-grandparents. No one knew for sure how far back his family had lived here. But Bernard's family were definitely Bostonians— and proud of it. Some of his relatives even went so far as to say that Boston <u>was the world</u>.

But Bernard had other ideas.

Bernard was a very inquisitive and adventurous mouse. He explored his home from the top of the attic...

to the bottom of the basement. He knew every hidden corner and cranny in the big old brownstone house.

7

It was the big world globe in the corner of the library that started Bernard wondering what it was like outside the old brownstone house. Once he started to wonder, Bernard began to read more and more. He wanted to find the answers.

He began to learn that in the world
outside his front door, exciting
and wonderful things were happening.
And he began to learn bigger
and bigger words.
"Am·ster·dam...cap·ti·vat·ing."
"Hong Kong...stim·u·lat·ing."
They made a singing sound when
he said them aloud.

11

Because Bernard was an adventurous mouse, as well as inquisitive, it wasn't long before he began to get an <u>itch</u> to see the world. "Father," said Bernard, "I want to go out and see the world."

"Not yet, Bernard," said his father. "You're still too young to leave home. Wait a bit."

"Oh, bother!" said Bernard.

"Switz·er·land…ex·hil·a·rat·ing."

"Af·ri·ca…fas·ci·nat·ing."

"France…de·lec·ta·ble."

"Someday," said Bernard, "I <u>am</u> going to see the world."

Bernard's father remembered when he
was a boy and had run away to become
a sailor. He had been about Bernard's age.

"Very well, Bernard, since you're so
set on seeing the world, I guess it
<u>is</u> time to let you go."

OUT INTO THE WORLD

"Hooray!" shouted Bernard.
"It's time. It's time for me
to go out into the world."

"But you must promise me one thing,"
said his father. "You must promise to
be back by Christmas Day. You know
how much your mother likes the family
together for the holidays. And besides,
Bernard, we'll need you to help put the
lights on the Christmas tree."

Bernard promised to return for
Christmas Day. And to Bernard,
a promise was a promise.

He packed a few belongings in his
knapsack. He kissed his mother and
father, and his three sisters, and
two brothers. With a wave, he left
the snug old brownstone house.

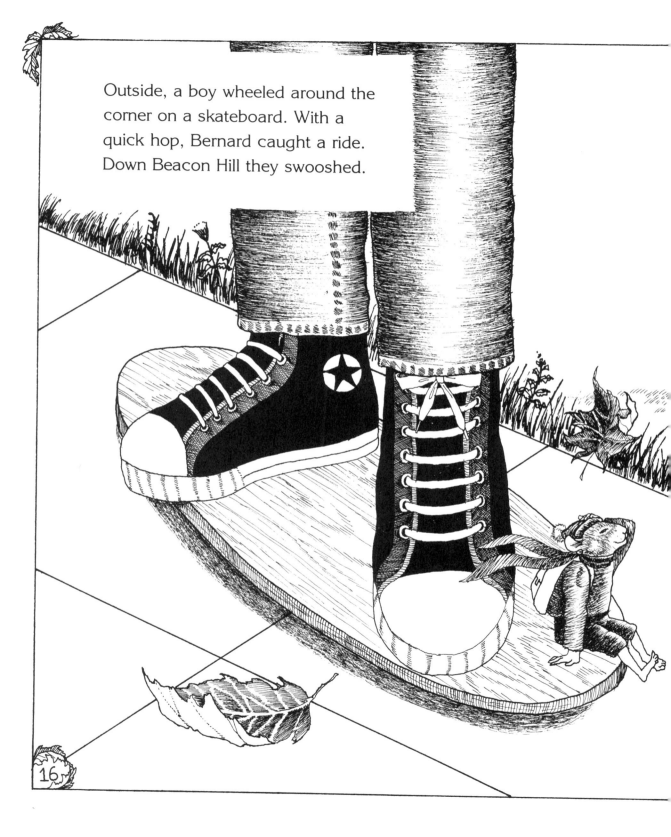

Outside, a boy wheeled around the corner on a skateboard. With a quick hop, Bernard caught a ride. Down Beacon Hill they swooshed.

It was a beautiful fall day but
there was a crispness in the air,
and Bernard was glad that he had put
on the cap and scarf that his mother
had made for him.

At the bottom of the hill the skateboard
stopped. Bernard caught a ride in the
basket of a friendly bicycle rider.
They rode through Boston Common and
the Public Garden.

17

Overhead, red and yellow leaves
fluttered against a blue sky.
Swan boats floated lazily across the pond.
"How cap·ti·vat·ing," said Bernard.

18

They rode down Commonwealth Avenue.
There were people walking,
and people riding
    ...in cars
    ...and buses
    ...on motor scooters
    ...and bicycles.
Everyone seemed to have someplace to go.
"How stim·u·lat·ing!" said Bernard.

19

They came to Charles River and turned down a path. On the river, boys rowed long boats. The college rowing teams were training in their shells. One passed close. Before Bernard thought twice, there he sat, in the shell, behind the coxswain.

"STROKE—and—STROKE—and—STROKE," shouted the coxswain. The long shell skimmed over the water.

The rowers pulled alongside a great ship.
"I could certainly see a lot of the world
from that ship," said Bernard. He caught
hold of a rope hanging over its side.
With a wave to the rowers, Bernard ran up
the rope and onto the deck of the ship.

Soon the ship's anchor lifted up and
away they sailed...out of the bay
...out into the ocean. The ship was a
passenger liner bound for Puerto Rico.

22

Bernard enjoyed the cruise. Every
so often he took a deep breath of
the good-smelling, salty ocean air.
"How in·vig·o·rat·ing!" he said.

But what he liked best on
board the ship was the food.
Fat, round cheeses from
all over the world.
Iced cakes
and cookies
and pies
and pastries
and pink-frosted petits fours.

UMMmm...de·lec·ta·ble!

Bernard explored the big ship, from the
engine room far below deck, to the crow's
nest high above. And of course he was
helpful. During a thick fog he climbed
up to the crow's nest to help keep watch.

He even helped the captain chart their course.

But by the time they reached the Florida
coast, Bernard was anxious to be on his way.
So when the liner docked at a port
in Florida, Bernard disembarked.

OUT INTO SPACE

There was a feeling of excitement
in the air. Bernard could sense it.
What was it? What was happening?

A car radio blared the news.
"The moon rocket will soon be
launched from Cape Canaveral."

"I have to see that," said Bernard.
A motorcycle sputtered close.
Bernard jumped up on the motorcycle.
Ahead a tall rocket jutted into the sky.
A guard stopped the motorcycle. "That's
as far as you can go," he said.
But no one paid any attention to Bernard
as he hurried off toward the huge rocket.

Out of a large van stepped three men.
"They must be the astronauts," said
Bernard. He moved closer. Each man
carried a small box with a cord attached
to his space suit. One of the men
stopped and set his box down. Bernard
had to get a better look at that box.
"How in·ter·est·ing," said Bernard. "There
are more buttons than on father's waistcoat."

The next thing he saw was the side of
the tall rocket sliding past. Bernard
was in an elevator going up—and up—
and up. Then he heard a voice counting:
10–9–8–7–6–5–4–3–2–1 VARROOOMMM!
Bernard was hurtling through space!
He couldn't believe it!
How had it happened?

He looked out the window at the bright
blue sky, and down at the fast-disappearing
earth far below. Bernard thought of his
mother and father, and his three sisters,
and two brothers—and the snug old
house on Beacon Hill.

"They weren't such bad kids,"
said Bernard. "Just high-spirited."

He looked down. "I always did want to see the world," said Bernard. "But I never thought I'd see it all at once."

He remembered the promise he had made to his father. But now he wondered if he would ever see his family and his home again. Bernard's throat felt as if he'd swallowed a hazelnut—shell and all.

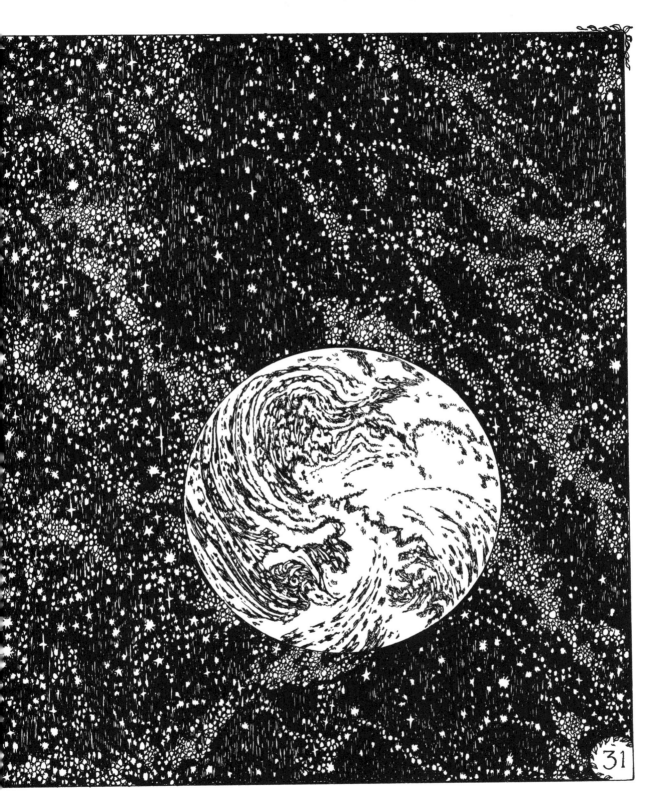

31

It was impossible for Bernard to stay worried for long. There were too many exciting things happening. He watched the astronauts taking pictures… reading instruments… talking to their base on earth. And it wasn't long before it was time to land on the moon.

Since Bernard was not wearing a space suit, he decided he'd better stay on board the spaceship.

Two of the astronauts climbed into a special vehicle that would take them to the moon. Off they went! Below, the moon looked like a vast, lonely desert.

"Good luck," said Bernard.

While the men explored the moon,
Bernard and the pilot circled around it.

When the astronauts returned to the spaceship, they brought several bulging sacks
back with them. Bernard took a closer
look at the sacks. "How curious," he said.
"I wonder what they found?"

Bernard became so absorbed in looking
out at space that he didn't even notice
when the rocket began its descent. Soon
the spaceship was rolling and bobbing.
Ocean waves sloshed against the windows.
They had splashed down!

Two frogmen tied lines from a helicopter
overhead to the spaceship. The ship
was carefully lifted into the air, and
gently set down on board an aircraft carrier.

The ship's bakers wheeled out a huge cake
with a tall sugar rocket on the top.
The captain congratulated the astronauts.

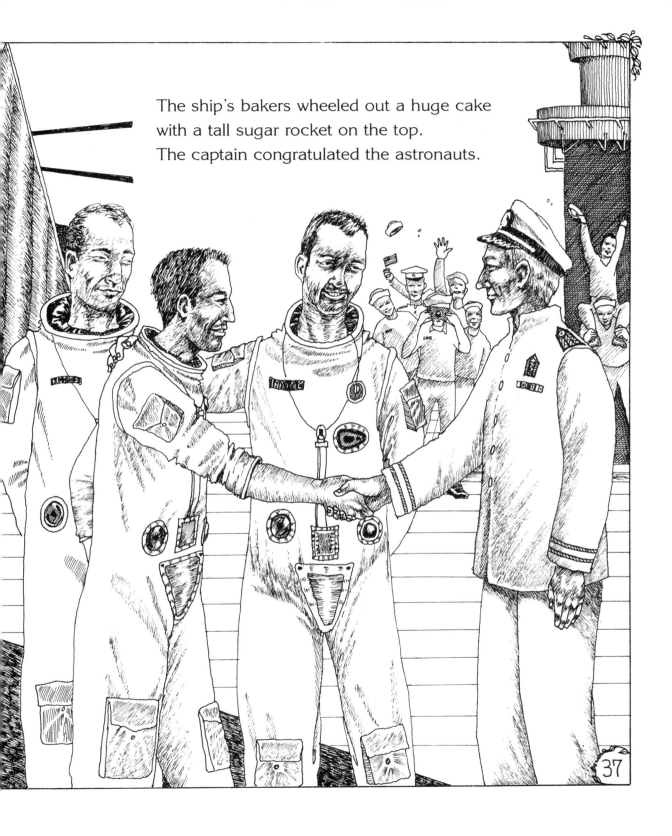

37

WELCOME HOME, BERNARD!

When it was time for the astronauts
to return to their base, of course
Bernard tagged along. And what with
one friendly ride—and another—
he finally got back to Massachusetts.

Bernard arrived in Boston
on the day before Christmas.

Snow was falling.

Bright-colored lights decorated the
trees in the Common and the Public
Garden. Christmas carolers, dressed
in costumes of long ago, sang songs.

Last-minute shoppers with gaily wrapped
packages hurried down the streets.
A spirit of joy and goodwill filled the air.

"Merry Christmas! Merry Christmas!" called passersby.

The brownstone house on Beacon Hill looked just the same as when Bernard had left. Only now a pine bough wreath hung on the front door, and soft candle lights shone from the windows.

How good to be home!

His mother and father, and his three sisters, and two brothers were very happy to see him.

Bernard's back!

Hooray!

Bernard kept his promise—he put the lights on the Christmas tree. Then Bernard reached into his knapsack and took out something very special.

This year, on the topmost branch of the
Christmas tree, Bernard hung a moon rock.

Now Bernard doesn't often leave his home,
except for his afternoon walk to the Common
and the Public Garden.

Most of the time he sits in the library
curled up in his favorite chair by the
fireplace, reading a book. He is content.
He has seen the world—and more.

"Oh, bother!" said Bernard,
pulling a hair from the tip
of his tail to mark his place
in the book.

"I wonder what Australia is like
in the summertime?"